The Rich Cake Mystery

Elaine Pageler

High
Nov

D1417478

Cover Design and Interior Illustrations: Tina Cash

International Standard Book Number: 1-57128-062-6

0 9 8 7 6 5 4 3 2 1
2 1 0 9 8 7 6 5 4 3

You'll enjoy all the High Noon Books. Write for
a free full list of titles.

Contents

CHAPTER 1

Dinner at the Cafe

Brad's boss asked him to dinner. They would meet at a cafe. There was just one problem. He had asked Meg Green, too. Brad didn't like that. He worked with her every day. Did he have to see that pest at night, too?

That night Brad drove to Pepe's Cafe. It was on Riddle Street.

Pepe stood inside the door. Menus were in his hands. "Table for one?" he asked Brad.

"I'm going to meet Mr. Ross," Brad said.

"Then you're Brad Jones. Mr. Ross left a call for you. He can't get away from the News. You and Miss Green are to have dinner. It's his treat. He says you two work hard. You're to have fun tonight," Pepe told him.

Brad tried to smile. But this was not good news. How could he have fun with Meg? She was so bossy. She only talked about work.

Pepe led Brad to a table. "I like to read the Riddle Street stories in the News. You and Meg Green do them. Don't you?"

"Yes, she writes the stories. I take the pictures," Brad said.

Brad's table was near the dance floor. He sat down and looked around.

A man played a keyboard. A sign and a bowl sat close by. The sign said, "Music by Jock." The bowl was for tips.

Brad tapped his foot along with the music. He liked to dance. But dancing with Meg wouldn't be fun. She might try to lead.

Pepe walked toward him. Meg followed. She wore a long dress. There was a red ribbon in her hair. Brad had to admit she looked pretty.

Pepe pulled the chair out for Meg. She smiled and sat down. "Where's the boss?" she asked.

Brad told her about Mr. Ross. "He wants us to have fun," he said.

Meg grinned. "O.K.," she said.

The waiter walked over and nodded to Brad. Then he gave Meg a big smile. "My name is Lon. I'm your waiter tonight," he said.

Meg looked at the menu. "Everything looks good. I bet it's rich," she said.

Lon's smile widened. "Yes, you'll like it. Your dinner will be very rich," he said.

Dinner was fun. They talked and laughed and had a good time. Brad couldn't believe it. Meg wasn't bossy tonight. Had she changed?

Lon came over. He cleared away the dishes. "Now I'll bring the lady's cake," he said.

"I didn't order cake," Meg said.

"It comes with your dinner. And the cake is very good," Lon told her.

"Do I get cake, too?" Brad asked hopefully.

Lon shook his head. "I'll put the cake in a doggie bag," he said. Then he walked off.

"I really don't want cake," Meg said.

But Brad did. "I'll give you a ride home for the cake. Now let's dance," Brad told her.

Meg smiled. "It's a deal," she said.

She turned out to be a good dancer. They whirled around the floor. Brad could have danced longer. But it was time to go. So they started off the floor.

"Don't forget to tip Jock," Meg ordered.

Brad groaned. This was the same old bossy Meg. But the music had been good. So he stopped and dropped money in Jock's bowl.

A woman walked up. The ribbon in her hair looked like Meg's. She put money in the bowl.

Brad and Meg headed for the door.

Lon rushed after them. "Wait! Here's your doggie bag," he called.

Brad glanced up and spotted Pepe. He was watching them. A frown was on his face. Then he turned and walked toward Lon.

They took the doggie bag and went out to the car. Brad started driving away.

"There's Lon. He just raced out of the cafe. Now he's waving his hands," Meg said.

"Does he want us to stop?" Brad asked.

Meg shook her head. "I don't know why. He must be waving at someone else," she said.

CHAPTER 2

The Doggie Bag

Brad dropped Meg off. "Thanks for the cake," he told her.

Meg laughed. "I bet you eat it tonight," she said.

"Maybe I will," Brad said. He grinned and drove home.

Brad parked his car. Then he walked to his door and heard his phone ringing. The key was in his pocket. But it was hard to find. At last he found it and opened the door.

The phone stopped ringing. It must have been Meg. Perhaps she wanted to know about the cake. Or she had an idea for a story. His phone had recorded her call. So she could wait. Right now he wanted cake.

Brad got a fork. Then he opened the doggie bag. The cake looked good. It had three layers and lots of frosting. He took a bite.

"Mmmmmm," he sighed.

Lon had said it was rich. And it was. Brad took one more bite and another. He was getting to the back of the cake. The next bite had a lot of frosting.

"Crunch!" Brad's teeth bit something. It was hard.

"Ouch!" Brad yelled.

He pulled the hard thing out of his mouth. It felt like metal. Did it chip his tooth? He flung it in the doggie bag. Then he dashed to the mirror. No, his tooth was O.K.

"What was that?" Brad wondered.

He took the doggie bag to the sink and washed off the metal. It began to sparkle. Why, it was a ring!

Brad held it up. The ring was gold. It held a big flashing stone. Was it a diamond?

"How did it get in the cake?" Brad wondered.

Then he thought about the phone call. Could it be about the ring? Brad rushed over.

*Brad held it up. The ring was gold.
It held a big flashing stone.*

He turned on the recorder.

It was Meg. "Hi, Brad. Sorry you can't have your cake yet. Lon called. He gave us the wrong doggie bag. Ours has kitchen scraps. So don't open it. He's bringing over the right doggie bag. Bye," she said.

Brad frowned. The doggie bag didn't have scraps. It held Meg's cake. And there was a ring in it. Why did Lon lie?

A knock sounded on the door. That must be Lon now.

Brad walked to the door. But he didn't open it. "Who is it?" he called.

"It's Lon. I have your cake," a voice called.

Brad stalled for time. "My cake?" he asked.

"Yes, the lady said she gave it to you. There was a mix-up. I gave you the wrong doggie bag. It has kitchen scraps. Give it to me. Then I'll give you the cake," Lon called.

Brad paused. Why didn't Lon say to throw away the scraps? Did he know about the ring?

"I don't have that doggie bag," Brad said. That wasn't a lie. He didn't have scraps.

"But the lady said you did," Lon said. His voice sounded alarmed.

Brad needed time to check this out. So he made up a story. "I didn't want the cake. So I threw it away when Meg wasn't looking," he said.

Lon gasped. "You did! Where did you

throw it?" he asked.

"I put it in a garbage can," Brad told him.

"What garbage can?" Lon asked.

"It's in front of the cafe," Brad said.

Lon forgot to give Brad the doggie bag he had brought. He didn't even say goodbye. Brad could hear him running away.

Yes, Lon knew about the ring. Did he put it there? Why would anyone put a ring in a cake? This was a real riddle.

"A riddle on Riddle Street," Brad thought.

Tomorrow he would tell Meg. Who knows? Maybe they could solve it. This might be their next story.

CHAPTER 3

The Diamond Ring

The ring sparkled even brighter the next day. It looked like a diamond. Brad put it in his pocket. Then he headed to work.

An idea popped into his head. Brad didn't stop at the News. He drove down to the cafe.

It was just as Brad thought. The sidewalk was a mess. Someone had gone through the garbage can. It lay on its side. Garbage was all over.

"Lon looked for the ring," Brad said. He turned and drove back to the News.

Meg sat at her desk. She smiled as he came in. "Did Lon bring over the doggie bag? I bet you ate the cake. Was it good?" she asked.

"It was rich," Brad said.

He held the ring in front of her nose. It sparkled in the light.

"Very rich," he added.

Meg's eyes flew open. "Where did you get that?" she gasped.

"This ring was in the cake. That's why it was so rich," Brad told her.

"I don't understand," Meg said.

Brad told her about the cake and the ring. He told her about Lon's visit and the garbage can, too.

"It's a real riddle. Why was the ring in the cake?" Brad asked.

A smile crossed Meg's face. "I know. Lon has a girlfriend. He wants to give her a ring. So he puts it in a piece of cake. Isn't that sweet?" she asked.

Brad frowned at Meg. She would think of something silly like that. "No, it isn't sweet. That ring could chip a tooth," Brad told her.

"Poor Lon. He doesn't know where the ring is. You should phone him," Meg went on.

Brad shook his head. "Why didn't Lon tell the truth? Something is wrong. We need more facts. Let's go to a jewelry store. They could tell us about this ring," he said.

Meg smiled. "O.K.," she said.

Bond's Jewelry Store was a block down Riddle Street. The owner looked up when they walked in. "May I help you?" he asked.

Brad pulled out the ring. He handed it to Mr. Bond. "Is this a real diamond?" he asked.

Mr. Bond looked at the ring. "Yes, it is. Where did you get this?" he asked.

Brad had to say something. "My aunt left it to me in her will," he said.

"Yes, it's a real diamond. Your aunt must have been rich. This is a very good ring," Mr. Bond said.

"What is it worth?" Brad asked.

"About $5,000," Mr. Bond said.

"$5,000!" Brad gasped.

Mr. Bond nodded. He looked at Meg's hand. It's much too big for your girlfriend. Shall I make the ring smaller?" he asked Brad.

Brad's face turned red. "No," he said.

Meg giggled.

Brad took the ring and turned toward the door. He almost ran into a woman. She was coming in the door.

Brad glanced back at her. Then he followed Meg outside. "So much for your idea. Lon didn't buy that ring for a girl. A waiter doesn't make that much money," he said.

Meg wouldn't give in. "Maybe a rich aunt left it to him," she said.

CHAPTER 4

Pepe's Cafe

Brad and Meg headed back up Riddle Street. They were still talking about the diamond. Then Brad spotted someone behind them.

"A man is following us," he told Meg.

The News was close by. They ducked inside and peeked out. The man stopped and stared at the door. It was Lon. He waited there. Then he walked across the street to a car. Another man was in it. But Brad and Meg couldn't see who it was.

Meg watched them drive off. "Sure, Lon was following us. We have his diamond," she said.

"The cake was baked at Pepe's Cafe. Someone put the ring inside. Lon knows about it. But is it his ring? I need more facts. Also, who was the other man in the car?" Brad asked.

Meg reached for the phone. "Then we'll do a story about Pepe's Cafe. Lon will be there. We can talk to him," she said.

Pepe asked them over at 5 o'clock. Brad had his camera. Meg carried a notebook. The story pleased Pepe. He led them through the cafe. Meg took notes. Brad snapped pictures.

Then Pepe led them to the kitchen. A woman and three men were inside. One of them was Lon.

He didn't seem happy to see them.

Pepe went on talking. "Come and meet my workers. This is my wife. She's the cook. Jock plays the music. Bob and Lon are the waiters. The five of us run the cafe," he said.

Everyone looked up and smiled except Lon. He looked at the floor.

Brad looked over at Lon. "Thank you for bringing over the cake," he said.

The room got very quiet. Everyone looked at Lon.

Pepe frowned. "What cake?" he asked.

Lon's eyes darted toward him. "The lady didn't eat her cake. I gave her the wrong doggie bag. So I took over the right one," he said.

Pepe turned to Brad and Meg. "Lon is new. He's only been here four days. A new waiter makes mistakes," he said.

Meg shot a quick glance at Brad. Then she smiled at Pepe. "Lon is a good waiter. He's cute, too. I bet he has a girlfriend. Was she here last night?" she asked.

Jock looked up and laughed. "So that's why he asked me to play love songs. I bet she was the cute girl in the back of the room. Is that right, Lon?" he asked.

Lon looked at Jock and nodded. Then he jumped up. "I hear the garbage truck. These waste baskets had better be emptied," he said.

Brad followed him out the back door and

took a picture. Getting rid of garbage was part of running a cafe, too.

Pepe called to him. "It's time for us to open. I'll take you and Meg to your table. Spend the evening here. This treat is on me. Take all the pictures you need," he said.

Again their table was near the dance floor. But Lon wasn't their waiter. Instead the other waiter came over. He gave them menus.

Meg looked at the menu. "There's the dinner I ordered last night. Dessert doesn't come with it. So why did Lon give me the cake?" she asked.

"I'd like to know that, too. Something is wrong," he told her.

CHAPTER 5

A Gang of Robbers

The next morning Brad went straight to the photo lab. Things on his desk could wait. He wanted to work on the pictures of Pepe's Cafe.

At last they were done. Brad put them in his pocket. Then he stepped out the lab door. There stood Meg. A letter was in her hand.

"Guess what? I found this on your desk. It's a note from Lon," Meg told him.

Brad reached for the letter. "Lon could have talked to us last night," he said.

There stood Meg. A letter was in her hand.

A small note was inside.

Dear Brad and Meg,

I know you have my ring. It was for my girl. She was at the cafe. You might have seen her. She sat near to the back. Her hair is black. She is about the size of Meg. Please give the ring back.

Lon

Brad looked at Meg. Now she would insist he give back the ring.

But she didn't. Instead Meg shook her head. "Lon is lying. His girl was my size. So he didn't buy the ring for her. Remember what Mr. Bond said. It would be too big," she said.

"But I still think he put the ring in the cake.

Maybe he stole it," Meg went on.

"We could check with the police. They might know if a diamond has been stolen," Brad said.

Meg glanced out the window. "Do you think Lon is still following us?" she asked.

"We'll go out the back door," Brad said.

Sergeant Ward was glad to see them. He looked at the ring and listened to what they had to say.

"Someone has been breaking into houses. This has been going on the last two weeks. It has to be more than one person. We think it's a gang of smart robbers. They have a way to get rid of stolen things," Sergeant Ward said.

"Was a diamond stolen?" Meg asked.

Sergeant Ward looked at his papers. "Yes, there was a robbery three nights ago. They took two TVs, a VCR, and a diamond ring. The people say the ring is worth $5,000," he said.

"That's what Mr. Bond says this diamond is worth," Meg told him.

"The robbery happened the night before we were at the cafe," Brad added.

Sergeant Ward thought for a minute. "It seems to fit. Maybe Lon wasn't giving the ring to his girl. Maybe he was giving it to someone else. That person would get rid of it for him," he said.

"Lon thought I was that person. I wonder

why?" Meg asked.

"I don't know. First, let's make sure this is the ring. The owners are here now. I'll show them the diamond. Stay here. I'll be right back," Sergeant Ward said.

Brad thought about his pictures. He put them out on the sergeant's desk.

Meg reached for one of them. "We've seen that woman before. She was in Mr. Bond's jewelry store. He called her Elsa," she said.

Brad looked at the picture. Lon was in it, too. He was handing Elsa a doggie bag.

"Sure, I remember now. Elsa was in the cafe the first night, too. I saw her tip Jock. She wore a red ribbon. It was just like your's," Brad said.

Meg's jaw dropped. "That's it! Lon thought I was her. He's new at the cafe. Someone gave him an order. Give the ring to the woman with a red ribbon," she said.

Brad got excited, too. "Lon gives jewelry to Elsa. She takes it to Mr. Bond. He sells it in his store," he said.

"That's right. Only Lon made a mistake. He gave the ring to me," Meg said.

Brad pointed to the picture. "But Elsa came to the cafe last night, too. Lon gave her a doggie bag. Was there another robbery? If so, it has jewelry inside," he told her.

Sergeant Ward came back in. There was a smile on his face. "It's the ring," he said.

Brad pointed to the pictures. He told about Elsa, the doggie bag, and Mr. Bond.

Sergeant Ward scanned the pictures. "The gang works out of the cafe. Now we know how they get rid of jewelry. But what happens to the TVs and VCRs?" he asked.

His eyes stopped at a picture. Brad had taken it outside. It showed cans and boxes and the garbage truck. A name was on the side.

"I know all the garbage companies in town. This isn't one of them," Sergeant Ward said.

"The other stolen things are put in the garbage. This truck picks them up," Brad added.

Sergeant Ward smiled. "I think we've found the robbers. They're at Pepe's Cafe," he said.

CHAPTER 6

Sergeant Ward's Plan

Brad and Meg sat in the sergeant's office. So did some other policemen. Sergeant Ward was talking to them.

"Lon is one of the robbers. They're at Pepe's Cafe. Five people work there. But we don't know how many are in the gang," he said.

"Lon followed Meg and me. There was a man waiting in the car. He must have known about the ring, too," Brad told him.

"We couldn't see who it was," Meg added.

"It must have been the leader. My guess is that it's Pepe. But we don't know for sure," Sergeant Ward replied.

A shocked look covered Meg's face. "Not Pepe! He's such a nice man," she said.

"I think so, too. But remember his face when we left that night. He saw the doggie bag and he wasn't happy," Brad said.

"That's true. And Pepe called you in from the back of the cafe. Maybe he didn't want you to see the garbage truck," Meg agreed.

"It sounds like he's the leader. I have a plan to catch him. Brad and Meg will give Lon the diamond. The owners will let us use the ring to catch the robbers," Sergeant Ward said.

"How about us? What do we do?" one of the policemen asked.

"Two of you watch Pepe's. The other two watch Bond's Jewelry Store. Here's what I think will happen. Lon will take the ring back to the cafe. Someone will phone Elsa. It's still early morning. She will go to Pepe's for lunch," Sergeant Ward said.

Brad cut in. "The ring will be in a doggie bag for her," he said.

"That's right. Elsa will take it to the jewelry store. Mr. Bond will pay her and give her money for the robbers. Tonight she will take it back to Pepe's. That when we close in and find out who the leader is," Sergeant Ward told them.

Brad went to the phone and called Lon. "We got your note. Meg and I both agree. We should give back the diamond. Meet us at the News in an hour," he said.

Meg kept watch out the window. This time Lon was alone. "He's coming up now," she said.

Lon came through the door and walked toward them. A worried look was on his face. Then he spotted the diamond on Brad's desk and smiled.

"Thanks for giving back the ring. I've been saving money for a long time. At last I got enough money to buy it," he said.

"And you put it in her cake. What a sweet surprise," Meg gushed.

Lon's hand tightened over the ring. "I thought so. Then I got it mixed up with your cake. But everything is turning out all right," he said.

Brad watched him hurry away. Then he phoned Sergeant Ward. "Lon just left," he told him.

"We're in a car in front of your building. Yes, I see him now. He's getting into a car. No one is with him. We're going to tail him. I'll phone you back this afternoon," Sergeant Ward said.

Brad and Meg stayed close to their desks. At last Sergeant Ward phoned.

"Everything went the way I thought it would. Lon came back to Pepe's. One of my men was inside. He saw Pepe phone someone,"

Sergeant Ward told them.

"Pepe phoned Elsa," Brad said.

"We don't know for sure. He might have called another person. But someone called her. Elsa came to the cafe. She left with a doggie bag," Sergeant Ward answered.

"Did she go to the jewelry store?" Brad wanted to know.

"Yes, she left the doggie bag there. Mr. Bond gave her two checks. I think one was for her. The other would be for the leader of the gang. She'll take it to Pepe's tonight. My men and I will be there. We'll make the arrest. But I want you and Meg there, too. We might need you," Sergeant Ward told him.

CHAPTER 7

The Arrest

Pepe was surprised to see Brad and Meg at the cafe that night. He smiled. But Brad wasn't sure the man was glad to see them.

"We need one more visit," Meg told him.

"Also, we like your food and Jock's music," Brad added.

Brad saw Elsa coming in the door. Pepe took them to a table. Then he went back and got her. Brad watched closely. Elsa did not hand Pepe anything.

Meg peeked around her menu. "Guess what? Lon is Elsa's waiter. He saw us and almost dropped his tray," she said.

"Will he be our waiter?" Brad asked.

Meg shook her head. "We get the other one. Sergeant Ward has men in here. I wonder who they are," she said.

Lon walked over to Elsa's table. He took her order. Then she handed him the menu. He started to walk away.

A man at the next table stood up quickly. He bumped into Lon and the menu fell to the floor. Nothing was inside.

"I'm sorry," the man said. He picked up the menu and handed it to Lon.

"That's a policeman," Brad said.

Lon made many trips to Elsa's table. Brad and Meg watched closely. Elsa didn't give him a check. The room was full by now. Jock played the keyboard. People ate and danced.

A man walked over to Elsa's table. He asked her to dance.

"We'll dance, too. But we don't need to watch Elsa. Pepe's people aren't on the dance floor," Brad said.

Elsa danced several times. So did Brad and Meg. Most people had left now.

Elsa put money on her bill and Lon carried it out to Pepe. Two men followed. So did Brad and Meg. This would be the check.

One of the men was Sergeant Ward. "Let me see that," he told Pepe.

Pepe frowned. "It's just the bill," he said.

"I think it's a check from Bond's Jewelry Store. It's for a stolen ring," Sergeant Ward said.

Pepe handed him the bill. "I don't know anything about a stolen ring. This is a bill and some money," he said.

Sergeant Ward looked at it. "The check isn't here. Search Elsa," he ordered.

The police searched her and found nothing. So they searched Pepe, his wife, Lon, and the other waiter, too. They even searched Pepe's desk and the kitchen. There was no check.

"There are no robbers here," Pepe said.

Sergeant Ward turned to Lon. "Where is the ring Brad gave you?" he asked.

"I gave it to my girl," Lon told him.

"I don't believe that. But we need that check. We can't hold anyone tonight without it," Sergeant Ward told his men.

Jock had been playing the keyboard. Now he stopped and stood up. "It's time to go home," he said.

Meg tugged on Brad's arm. "You should tip Jock," she said.

Meg was being bossy again. Brad started to get angry. Then he stopped. "Meg, you've got it. Elsa always tips Jock. That's where the check is," he said.

Brad grabbed Jock's bowl and tipped it over.

Brad grabbed Jock's bowl and tipped it over. Out rolled some money and a check. "Here's the gang leader. Isn't that right, Lon?" he asked.

"Be quiet!" Jock hissed.

Lon began talking. Yes, he helped Jock rob houses. But Jock was the leader. He got rid of everything through people who came to the cafe. Lon got a job there to help him. Pepe, his wife, and the other waiter knew nothing.

"My men will arrest Mr. Bond and the garbage driver, too. We've got the whole gang. Brad and Meg solved another case," Sergeant Ward said.

Brad smiled. "It was a piece of cake."

THE BOOK OF CROOKS

by MICHAEL ANTHONY STEELE

Illustrated by JASON ARMSTRONG
Color by LEE LOUGHRIDGE

BATMAN created by Bob Ka

D14

SCHOLASTIC INC

New York   Toronto   London   Aucklan
Mexico City   New Delhi   Hong Kong

No part of this publication may be reproduced in whole or in part, or stored in a retrieval system,
or transmitted in any form or by any means, electronic, mechanical, photocopying, recording, or
otherwise, without written permission of the publisher. For information regarding permission, write to
Scholastic Inc., Attention: Permissions Department, 557 Broadway, New York, NY 10012.

ISBN 0-439-72780-4

Designed by Heather Barber

Batman and all related characters: TM & © 2005 DC Characters, Inc. Batman, the television show:
© 2005 Warner Bros. Entertainment, Inc. All Rights Reserved.

Published by Scholastic Inc. SCHOLASTIC and associated logos are trademarks and/or registered trademarks of
Scholastic Inc.

12 11 10 9 8 7 6 5 4 3 2 1   5 6 7 8 9 10/0

Printed in the U.S.A. First printing, September 2005

Gotham City. Three years ago, its towering statues and gothic architecture loomed over crime-ridden streets. The shadows ran long and deep, harboring the criminal element below.

That was then.

Now, Gotham has one of the lowest crime rates in the nation. What caused such a plummet in corruption? A booming economy? An increased police force? Stricter laws decreed by city hall?

None of those things.

Exactly three years ago, a dark knight began a personal crusade against crime. A crime fighter known as . . .

A mysterious figure rarely glimpsed by the average citizen, Batman is the last person any criminal wants to encounter. He has dedicated his life to bringing law to the lawlessness of Gotham. He is the soldier in a one-man war against crime and corruption.

Batman's true identity is Bruce Wayne, heir to the multibillion dollar Wayne fortune. Bruce's normal life ended one dreary night long ago when a gun-toting hoodlum murdered his parents in front of him. Since then, young Bruce Wayne has dedicated his life to fighting crime in any form it takes.

Knowing that criminals are cowardly and superstitious, Bruce designed Batman's appearance so it would strike terror in the hearts of the heartless. He developed and uses a wide array of weapons and tactics to capture his prey and deliver them to justice. His skill and training make him seem to appear everywhere at once and nowhere at all. To be a criminal in Gotham means to constantly keep a lookout over your shoulder for a dark, vengeful shape leaping from the shadows.

Thanks to Bruce Wayne, Batman has taken back the night in Gotham City.

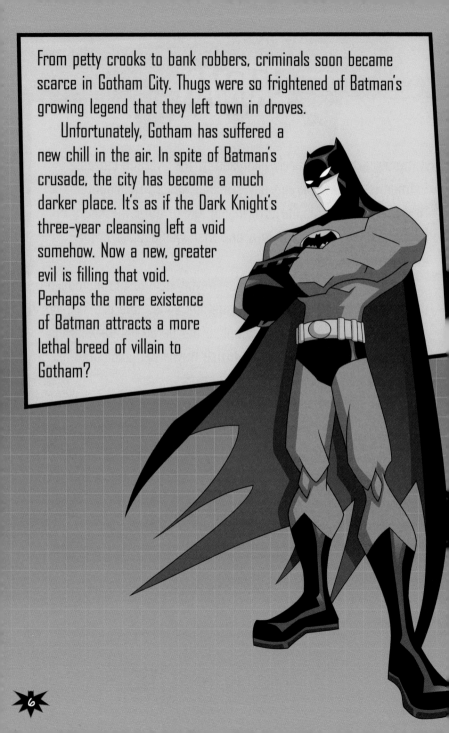

From petty crooks to bank robbers, criminals soon became scarce in Gotham City. Thugs were so frightened of Batman's growing legend that they left town in droves.

Unfortunately, Gotham has suffered a new chill in the air. In spite of Batman's crusade, the city has become a much darker place. It's as if the Dark Knight's three-year cleansing left a void somehow. Now a new, greater evil is filling that void. Perhaps the mere existence of Batman attracts a more lethal breed of villain to Gotham?

The following pages contain a rogues' gallery of the most diabolical criminals in Gotham. Some have territorial claims on the city while others have psychotic fixations on Batman himself. Their schemes range from making themselves rich to satisfying their undying need for mayhem. Some are misguided or simply deranged. Others are evil masterminds hatching schemes of domination. A few are completely insane. No matter how they're characterized, these flamboyant felons represent the new breed of criminals in Gotham City.

THE PENGUIN

Real Name:
OSWALD COBBLEPOT

Height:
4'8"

Weight:
173 lbs.

Crimes:
Assault, burglary, kidnapping, and racketeering

Oswald Cobblepot, also known as Penguin, is a rare bird among Gotham's supercriminals. Born into a rich family, Penguin is rude, selfish, and arrogant. He serves as a mirror image of what Bruce Wayne could have become. However, Oswald has squandered his once immense family fortune. Now Penguin seeks to replenish his riches through criminal activities. He's a skilled burglar and ornithologist who sometimes uses birds to carry out his disreputable schemes. Armed with his birds, spiked umbrella, and two deadly assassins called the Kabuki Twins, he is a surprisingly skillful and dangerous foe.

MR. FREEZE

Real Name:
VICTOR FRIES

Height:
6' 4"

Weight:
181 lbs.

Crimes:
Robbery, assault, and destruction of property

Victor Fries was a petty criminal who was first noticed by Batman when he graduated to bank robbery. Batman's pursuit of Victor led them to a cryogenic suspension facility — a subzero storage warehouse. While trying to escape, the thief accidentally tumbled into a damaged cryo chamber. A bizarre mix of electricity and experimental coolants nearly killed Victor. Instead, it severely altered his body chemistry.

Victor is now Mr. Freeze, a dangerous criminal who can create sheets of ice by mere touch. No longer interested in banks, Mr. Freeze is after a different kind of "ice." He steals priceless diamonds, freezing solid all who stand in his way. But that's just the tip of the iceberg. If Mr. Freeze had his way, all of Gotham would be frozen.

FIREFLY

Real Name:
GARFIELD LYNNS

Height:
5'9"

Weight:
186 lbs.

Crimes:
Arson, vandalism, and corporate espionage

No sooner had Batman thawed out Gotham from Mr. Freeze when suddenly he had to keep it from going up in flames. A rash of arsons brought the Dark Knight face-to-face with an airborne criminal calling himself Firefly.

From the large yellow lenses on his helmet to the bulbous energy tank of his jet pack, every part of his flight suit is modeled after a large insect.

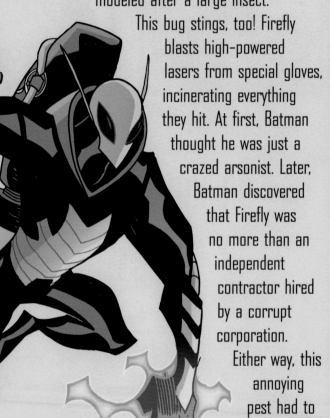

This bug stings, too! Firefly blasts high-powered lasers from special gloves, incinerating everything they hit. At first, Batman thought he was just a crazed arsonist. Later, Batman discovered that Firefly was no more than an independent contractor hired by a corrupt corporation. Either way, this annoying pest had to be swatted.

MAN-BAT

Real Name:
DR. KIRK LANGSTROM

Height:
5'6"

Weight:
172 lbs.

Crimes:
Assault, kidnapping, and animal cruelty

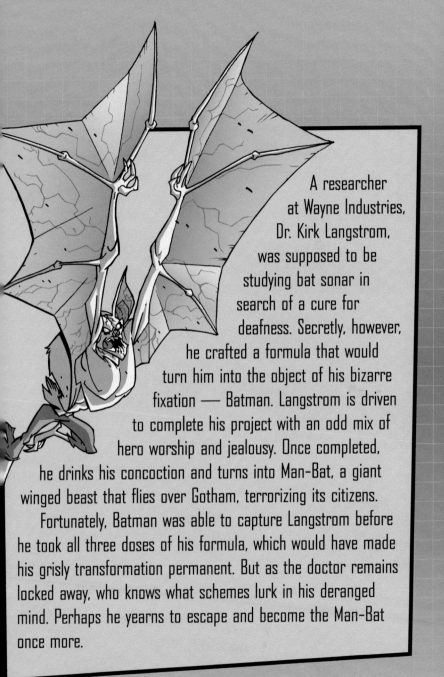

A researcher at Wayne Industries, Dr. Kirk Langstrom, was supposed to be studying bat sonar in search of a cure for deafness. Secretly, however, he crafted a formula that would turn him into the object of his bizarre fixation — Batman. Langstrom is driven to complete his project with an odd mix of hero worship and jealousy. Once completed, he drinks his concoction and turns into Man-Bat, a giant winged beast that flies over Gotham, terrorizing its citizens.

Fortunately, Batman was able to capture Langstrom before he took all three doses of his formula, which would have made his grisly transformation permanent. But as the doctor remains locked away, who knows what schemes lurk in his deranged mind. Perhaps he yearns to escape and become the Man-Bat once more.

VENTRILOQUIST AND SCARFACE

Real Name:
ARNOLD WESKER

Height:
5'7"

Weight:
185 lbs.

Crimes:
Assault, robbery, and racketeering

Although Arnold Wesker may seem like a quiet, timid man, he's no dummy. On the other hand, his boisterous sidekick, Scarface, is just that. Psychologically unsound, Wesker suppressed so much of his feelings over the years that multiple personalities soon emerged. The most dominant of these is Scarface, a ruthless gang leader with a taste for lawlessness.

It is often difficult to see who is really pulling the strings. Ventriloquist is quick to admit that Scarface is in charge and Wesker himself is the mere puppet. Batman had to face that very dilemma when Ventriloquist created a giant-sized, robotic version of Scarface. Wesker rode in the crook of Scarface's giant arm while the dummy went on a rampage through the city.

RIDDLER

Real Name:
EDWARD NIGMA

Height:
6'1"

Weight:
182 lbs.

Crimes:
Extortion, destruction of property, and grand larceny

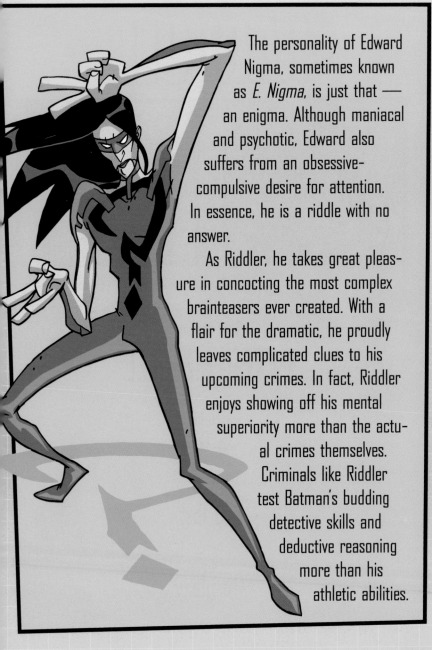

The personality of Edward Nigma, sometimes known as *E. Nigma*, is just that — an enigma. Although maniacal and psychotic, Edward also suffers from an obsessive-compulsive desire for attention. In essence, he is a riddle with no answer.

As Riddler, he takes great pleasure in concocting the most complex brainteasers ever created. With a flair for the dramatic, he proudly leaves complicated clues to his upcoming crimes. In fact, Riddler enjoys showing off his mental superiority more than the actual crimes themselves. Criminals like Riddler test Batman's budding detective skills and deductive reasoning more than his athletic abilities.

RAGDOLL

Real Name:
PETER MERKEL

Height:
5'6"

Weight:
170 lbs.

Crimes:
Burglary

Merkel was born with hyper-elastic tendons and ligaments. This allows him to twist and contort in a variety of different ways. Being "triple-jointed," Merkel is able to squeeze through almost any opening, no matter how small.

His unique abilities make him an excellent thief. As Ragdoll, he's able to get in and out of most secure areas without a trace. His abilities also allow him to stow away in the most cramped quarters. There he can hide and simply wait for the opportunity to escape with his prize.

In battle, Ragdoll can withstand massive amounts of punishment. He's extremely difficult to capture and much harder to hold onto. Batman had to modify his fighting styles to take down this twisted criminal.

CLAYFACE

Real Name:
DETECTIVE
ETHAN BENNETT

Height:
6'1"

Weight:
195 lbs.

Crimes:
Assault, destruction of property, and burglary

Ethan Bennett had been one of Bruce Wayne's best friends since college. So no one was more shocked than Batman when he witnessed his friend swallow a toxic formula that would change his life forever. The solution was a powerful solvent that breaks down anything into a malleable, rubbery substance. Suddenly Ethan's entire body could be molded like clay into almost any form imaginable.

Calling himself Clayface, Ethan can shape shift to resemble another person entirely, or he can transform his hands into giant hammers during battle. Between the formula's effect on his mind and his rage of vengeance, Ethan Bennett is slowly disappearing and Clayface is taking over.

Sadly, Batman has to watch as he slowly loses a dear friend.

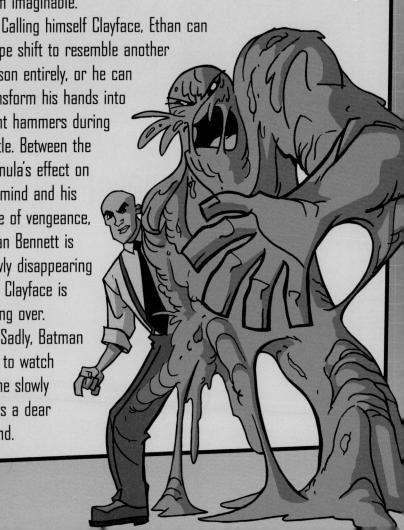

CLUEMASTER

Real Name:
ARTIE BROWN

Height:
5'4"

Weight:
356 lbs.

Crimes:
Kidnapping

Artie Brown was extremely intelligent even as a child. He was so smart that he was the reigning champion on a quiz show when he was only thirteen. However, after the embarrassment of a bitter defeat, Artie closed himself off to the world. He grew up to become a resentful and inactive man.

In order to get his revenge, Artie assumed the identity of the Cluemaster. As the hefty supervillain, he tracked down and kidnapped several people. Those people just happened to be the contestants who defeated him on that quiz show over two decades ago. He took over a television station and planned to humiliate them just like he was humiliated so long ago.

Fearing the Cluemaster would harm his prisoners, Batman had to track him down by unraveling the cryptic clues he left behind.

KILLER CROC

Real Name:
WAYLON JONES

Height:
6'9"

Weight:
244 lbs.

Crimes:
Assault, robbery, and racketeering

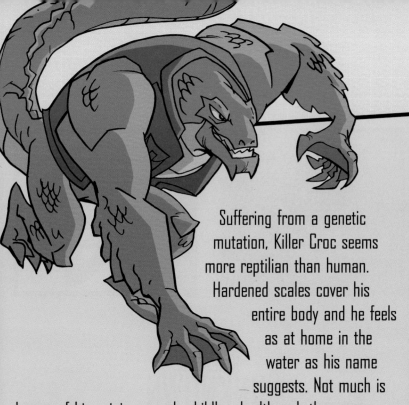

Suffering from a genetic mutation, Killer Croc seems more reptilian than human. Hardened scales cover his entire body and he feels as at home in the water as his name suggests. Not much is known of his origin or early childhood, although there are rumors about him growing up in a seedy circus sideshow, so it's not too surprising that he has turned to crime.

Keeping to the swamps near Gotham and the sewers beneath it, Killer Croc was an elusive crime boss. However, if Batman wasn't around to stop him, the Croc would have flooded all of Gotham, making it more like his preferred habitat.

Killer Croc's mutated body can withstand many different attacks. So, once again, Batman had to create a brand-new plan of attack in order to stop the raging reptile from brutally muscling his way into the city.

BANE

Real Name:
UNKNOWN

Height:
8'11"

Weight:
428 lbs.

Crimes:
Assault, destruction of property, and random violence

Little is known about this deadly mercenary. What is known is that in a secret lab, deep in the Amazon jungle, he had volunteered for experimental physical enhancements. These enhancements greatly magnify his strength with a chemical-neural infusion. With a touch to the controller on the back of his head, Bane floods his bloodstream with a modified steroid solution. The solution allows Bane to bulk up to three times his normal size and strength.

Bane was originally brought to Gotham at the request of the dwindling crime lords. His single assignment was to break the Bat. Bane turned out to be more than a match for Batman in terms of raw strength and toughness. In combat, Bane sorely tests Batman's fighting skills, nearly putting an end to his crime-fighting career. Batman was forced to rely on guile, wits, and a specially designed Bat-Bot before he could triumph over Bane.

SPELLBINDER

Real Name:
IRA BILLINGS

Height:
5'9"

Weight:
210 lbs.

Crimes:
Burglary

Ira Billings is a master of super-hypnosis. As Spellbinder, he is able to force others to do things against their will. His victims will often commit crimes on his behalf while he is safely out of harm's way and clear from suspicion.

Batman first discovered Spellbinder's wicked ways when priceless heirlooms went missing among many of Gotham's wealthiest citizens. At first, it seemed as if each of their butlers was pilfering their priceless possessions. When Bruce Wayne's own butler, Alfred, did the same, Batman knew something was wrong. He had to keep a sound mind to keep from falling under Spellbinder's spell.

HENCHMEN, GOONS, AND ASSASSINS

Not every crook Batman faces is a supervillain, although some are just as deadly. Many of the smalltime hoods who didn't leave Gotham decided to work for some of the bigger criminals. Little did they know that their bosses would gladly abandon them in order to save their own worthless skins.

At first, the goons working for the Ventriloquist were amused by his commanding dummy. They didn't care as long as they were paid. If they only knew just how dangerous that little dummy would turn out to be!

Sammy and Freddy overlook their boss's ghastly appearance. If anyone is mean enough to defeat Batman and take over Gotham City, they think it will be Killer Croc.

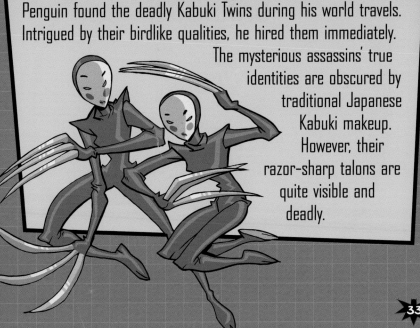

Penguin found the deadly Kabuki Twins during his world travels. Intrigued by their birdlike qualities, he hired them immediately. The mysterious assassins' true identities are obscured by traditional Japanese Kabuki makeup. However, their razor-sharp talons are quite visible and deadly.

SOLOMON GRUNDY

Real Name:
UNKNOWN

Height:
7'4"

Weight:
286 lbs.

Crimes:
Burglary

Legend has it that Solomon Grundy is the avenging spirit of Syrus Gold, a man who was murdered and dumped into the swamps outside Gotham in 1894. This monstrous behemoth gets his name from an old nursery rhyme containing the phrase, "Solomon Grundy, born on Monday. . . ."

One Halloween, the legend seemed to become reality. Grundy wandered into Gotham to take revenge on the descendants of Gold's murderers. Batman quickly revealed Grundy to be Clayface. He had assumed the creature's form and legend as a cover for a looting spree. Although the legend of Solomon Grundy remains just a legend, who knows what really lurks in Gotham's murky swamps?

CATWOMAN

Real Name:
SELINA KYLE

Height:
5'7"

Weight:
120 lbs.

Crimes:
Burglary

When this cat first entered the scene, the Gotham police mistook her for an associate of Batman. Her methods, stealth, and attire seemed too similar to be a coincidence. However, Catwoman is no crime fighter. She is Selina Kyle, a skillful cat burglar with a taste for priceless feline art. She steals from Gotham's wealthiest citizens not only to maintain her lavish lifestyle but for the adrenaline rush she gets during her adventures.

Although she sometimes helps Batman, she remains on the wrong side of the law. Unfortunately, he has never been able to catch her. Using her eight-foot bullwhip to scale rooftops, this cat always seems to land on her feet. Batman always takes special care when going after her. When backed into a corner, this kitty has claws.

JOKER

Real Name:
UNKNOWN

Height:
6' 4"

Weight:
181 lbs.

Crimes:
Robbery, assault, and destruction of property

The clown prince of crime, Joker is a complete madman. His mind is a place of thick and twisted horrors. His appearance echoes that very madness with spiked green hair, permanent pallid makeup, and an eternally evil grin. His maniacal plots rarely make any logical sense. Whether he's kidnapping a single victim or terrorizing the entire city, Joker always has a flair for the extravagant. He enjoys giving his schemes a *killer* punch line.

At first, Batman regarded the Joker as merely a crazed lunatic, psychologically ill and in need of treatment. Through their many encounters, however, Batman is becoming aware that this fiend may be his arch nemesis. As Joker puts it, he is the comedy to Batman's tragedy.

Ironically, Joker's first appear-ance was at the Arkham Asylum for the Criminally Insane. The madman began his crime spree by attacking the staff and releasing the asylum's mentally ill patients.

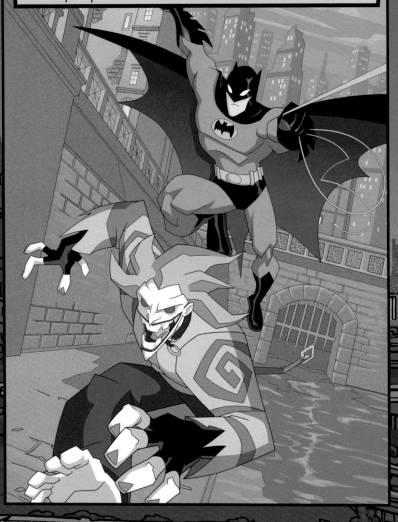

PROFESSOR HUGO STRANGE

Arkham Asylum is now the permanent residence for Joker along with many of the other supervillains captured by Batman. The new head psychiatrist, Professor Hugo Strange, cares for the dangerously deranged in hopes that they may one day be able to reenter society.

If an inmate escapes and returns to a life of crime, Batman will always be there to set things right. Yet, to catch these villains, it takes a special man behind the mask.

When Bruce Wayne's parents were murdered before his eyes, he vowed to avenge their deaths. Instead of living a life of violent vengeance, though, Bruce channeled his pain toward the pursuit of justice. With his family's wealth and resources, he attended the finest universities all over the world. When he finished school, the *real* learning began. He continued to travel the globe, becoming skilled in every fighting style and discipline imaginable. From the stealth of Japanese ninjas to the hunting skills of African Bushmen, Bruce mastered them all.

Three years ago, Bruce first donned the mantle of the bat and took to the rooftops of Gotham City. As he continues his crusade, he often struggles to maintain the balance between Batman and Bruce Wayne. The longer he fights this battle, the more Bruce begins to wonder if Batman is his true identity and Bruce Wayne is the mask.

WAYNE MANOR

Living in luxurious Wayne Manor, Bruce maintains the very visible lifestyle of Gotham's most eligible bachelor. His public persona is the complete opposite of the dark and mysterious Batman. He's laid back, stylishly dressed, and rarely serious enough to wear a tie, even to important board meetings. There's no way that anyone would connect the carefree Bruce Wayne to the legendary Dark Knight. That's just the way Bruce likes it.

WAYNE INDUSTRIES

As the somewhat honorary CEO of Wayne Industries, Bruce is finding less and less time to be involved in the business end of his family's legacy. He does, however, makes sure Wayne Industries contributes to the many charities and foundations he has established over the years. Little do they know, Wayne Industries also contributes much of its cutting-edge research and technology to Bruce's nocturnal activities.

The Wayne family butler, Alfred Pennyworth, cared for Bruce after he was orphaned. As the years passed, he helped the young Bruce Wayne immerse himself in his training to begin his crusade. To this day, Alfred acts as Bruce's valet, advisor, and best friend. He assists the young millionaire in everything from cooking his meals to instructing him on ways to better maintain his secret identity.

Well educated, Alfred's duties carry him above and beyond the usual job description for a butler. He helps maintain Batman's equipment and even acts as a medic on the crime fighter himself. Alfred cares very deeply for Bruce and always will be there for him. However, when Alfred is bandaging a wound or wrapping a sprain, he'll often try to discourage Bruce from his quest. He revels in Bruce's triumphs, but his defeats are difficult to bear.

45

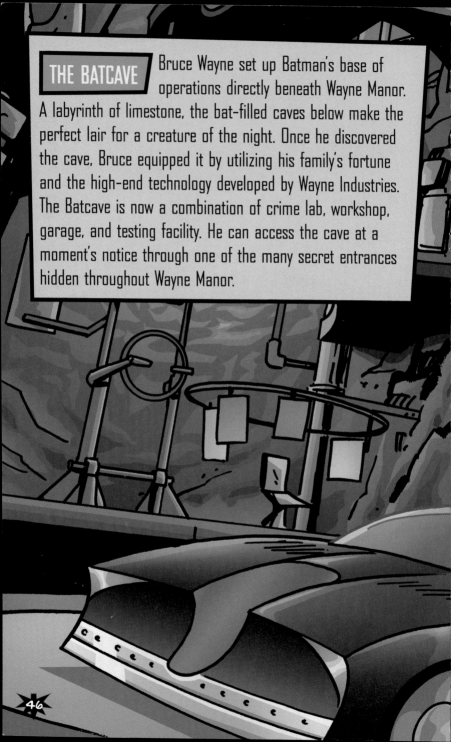

THE BATCAVE Bruce Wayne set up Batman's base of operations directly beneath Wayne Manor. A labyrinth of limestone, the bat-filled caves below make the perfect lair for a creature of the night. Once he discovered the cave, Bruce equipped it by utilizing his family's fortune and the high-end technology developed by Wayne Industries. The Batcave is now a combination of crime lab, workshop, garage, and testing facility. He can access the cave at a moment's notice through one of the many secret entrances hidden throughout Wayne Manor.

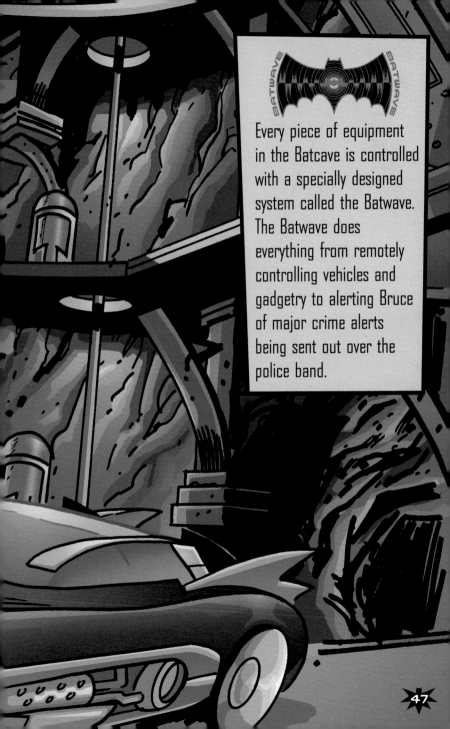

Every piece of equipment in the Batcave is controlled with a specially designed system called the Batwave. The Batwave does everything from remotely controlling vehicles and gadgetry to alerting Bruce of major crime alerts being sent out over the police band.

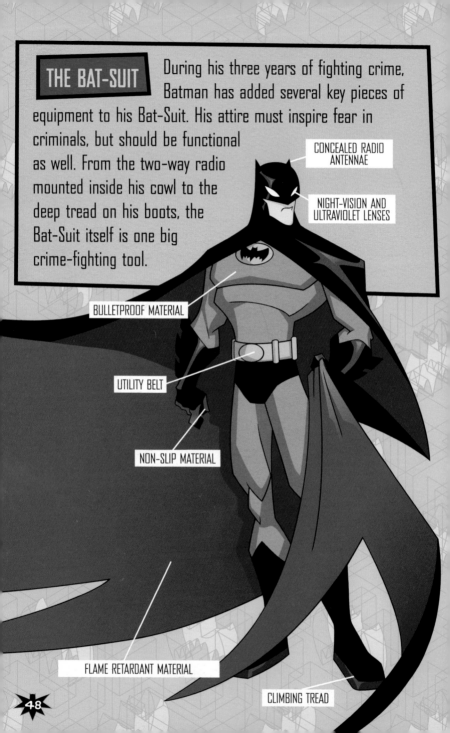

THE BAT-SUIT

During his three years of fighting crime, Batman has added several key pieces of equipment to his Bat-Suit. His attire must inspire fear in criminals, but should be functional as well. From the two-way radio mounted inside his cowl to the deep tread on his boots, the Bat-Suit itself is one big crime-fighting tool.

CONCEALED RADIO ANTENNAE

NIGHT-VISION AND ULTRAVIOLET LENSES

BULLETPROOF MATERIAL

UTILITY BELT

NON-SLIP MATERIAL

FLAME RETARDANT MATERIAL

CLIMBING TREAD

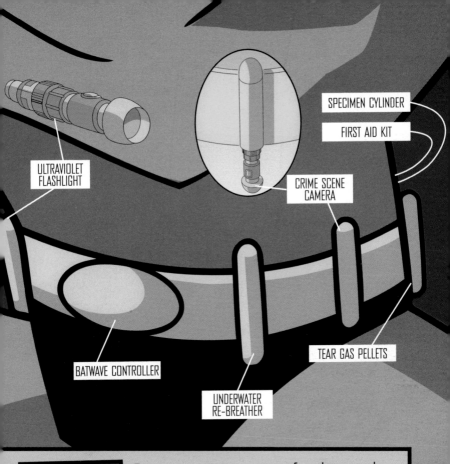

ULTRAVIOLET
FLASHLIGHT

SPECIMEN CYLINDER

FIRST AID KIT

CRIME SCENE
CAMERA

BATWAVE CONTROLLER

UNDERWATER
RE-BREATHER

TEAR GAS PELLETS

UTILITY BELT Batman carries an array of gadgets and tools inside his sophisticated utility belt. Leaving his hands free for scaling rooftops, the tiny storage compartments in his belt are specially designed to conceal the most useful of crime fighting devices and non-lethal weapons. The belt holds everything from tear gas pellets, used to disable enemies, to an Underwater Re-breather, which allows six minutes of breathable air. Batman will also customize his arsenal depending on the criminal he's hunting.

BATARANG™

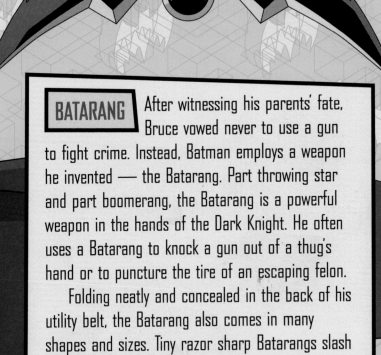

BATARANG After witnessing his parents' fate, Bruce vowed never to use a gun to fight crime. Instead, Batman employs a weapon he invented — the Batarang. Part throwing star and part boomerang, the Batarang is a powerful weapon in the hands of the Dark Knight. He often uses a Batarang to knock a gun out of a thug's hand or to puncture the tire of an escaping felon.

Folding neatly and concealed in the back of his utility belt, the Batarang also comes in many shapes and sizes. Tiny razor sharp Batarangs slash binding ropes while larger, self-propelled Batarangs can be maneuvered using Batman's special Batwave controller. A Batarang is even fired at the end of Batman's special grapnel.

GRAPNEL A dark shadow flying above the city streets serves to feed the growing legend of Batman. To create the illusion of flight, the Dark Knight uses a special grapnel that fires a wall-piercing Batarang. This allows him to swing from rooftop to rooftop on a thin, high-tension cable. The grapnel also includes a powerful retracting motor. It's capable of hoisting him straight off the ground — out of harm's way or into the fray.

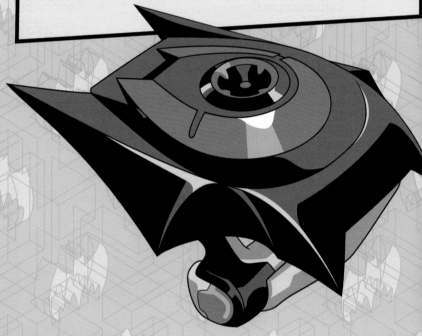

53

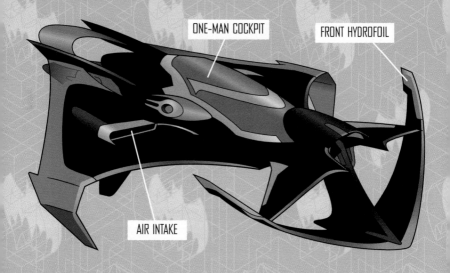

ONE-MAN COCKPIT

FRONT HYDROFOIL

AIR INTAKE

THE BATBOAT

Gotham is a coastal city and too often criminals expand their devious plans to include Gotham Harbor and beyond. Batman quickly discovered that he would have to travel by sea as well as by land. Thus the Batboat was created. Whether breaking up an arms smuggling ring or investigating a highjacking at sea, the Batboat speeds Batman to the scene of the crime.

More like a plane than a boat, the Batboat uses hydrofoil technology. Its high-powered propeller thrusts the Batboat along the sea while lifting its hull off the water's surface. This gives the Batboat the additional speed and maneuverability needed to chase even the fastest watercraft.

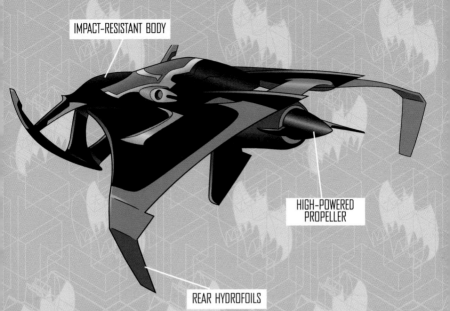

IMPACT-RESISTANT BODY

HIGH-POWERED
PROPELLER

REAR HYDROFOILS

THE BATCYCLE When the Batmobile is out of commission, or if a smaller vehicle fits the bill, Batman uses the Batcycle. This highly modified street bike doesn't trade speed for the ability to maneuver in and out of tight spaces.

Like the Batmobile, the Batcycle can be remotely driven using the Batwave.

OTHER BAT ACCESSORIES

As Batman faces new challenges and surprises, he must constantly update his tools and technology.

THE BATGLIDER AND JET PACK

When the ability to fly is needed, Batman employs a set of his specially designed wings. This winged jet pack allows its user to soar high above the Gotham rooftops with the maneuverability of a precision fighter jet, while the Batglider folds away for storage until an emergency flight situation arises.

POLAR BAT-SUIT

Sometimes Batman has to dress for success. When battling the bitter Mr. Freeze, Batman utilized one of his auxiliary Bat-Suits. This winterized costume is made of highly insulated material and shields Batman's entire face. It also comes equipped with two hand-held flamethrowers when it's time to heat things up.

BAT-BOT

Sometimes Batman's skill and combat training aren't enough. When more raw power is needed, Batman dons the Bat-Bot. This enormous, robotic exoskeleton gives Batman massive amounts of strength while protecting him from lethal blows. The Bat-Bot was instrumental in the eventual defeat of Bane.
Like most other Bat-vehicles, it too can be operated remotely using the Batwave.

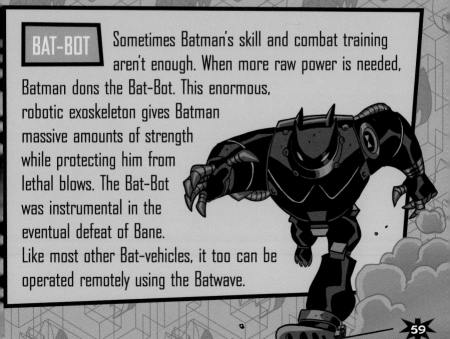

THE GOTHAM CITY POLICE DEPARTMENT

Publicly, the Chief of the Gotham City Police Department has gone on record stating that Batman is nothing more than an urban legend. Privately, the chief gave orders that this mysterious vigilante be found and brought to justice. Many of the officers themselves are suspicious of Batman's knack for showing up where crime is and the police aren't. Moreover, the mysterious crime fighter is something of a public relations problem. If crime has plummeted in the past three years, Gotham PD should be able to take the credit for it.

DETECTIVE ETHAN BENNETT

Ethan Bennett is a college friend of Bruce Wayne and a secret fan of Batman. Although he sometimes questions the crime fighter's motives, Ethan is glad that it's safe to walk the city streets at night again. He knows his duty — if given the chance, he would reluctantly bring in Batman. Thankfully, he doesn't think that chance will ever come.

DETECTIVE ELLEN YIN

Transferred from Metropolis, Detective Yin was brought in specially to track down the Bat. At first, she doesn't share Ethan Bennett's admiration of the Dark Knight. She wanted him brought in no matter how many crooks he took off the streets. He functions outside the law and that was enough to condemn him. However, after being forced to work more closely with the Caped Crusader, she is beginning to gain respect for him.

61

In the end, it doesn't matter what the police think of Batman. It doesn't matter if the public even believes in him. What matters is that he will continue his crusade against crime. He will help those in need and bring to justice those who need to be judged.

He will battle enemies using every ounce of strength in his body. He will track down villains using every skill and resource at his disposal.

As long as there is crime in Gotham City, there will always be . . .